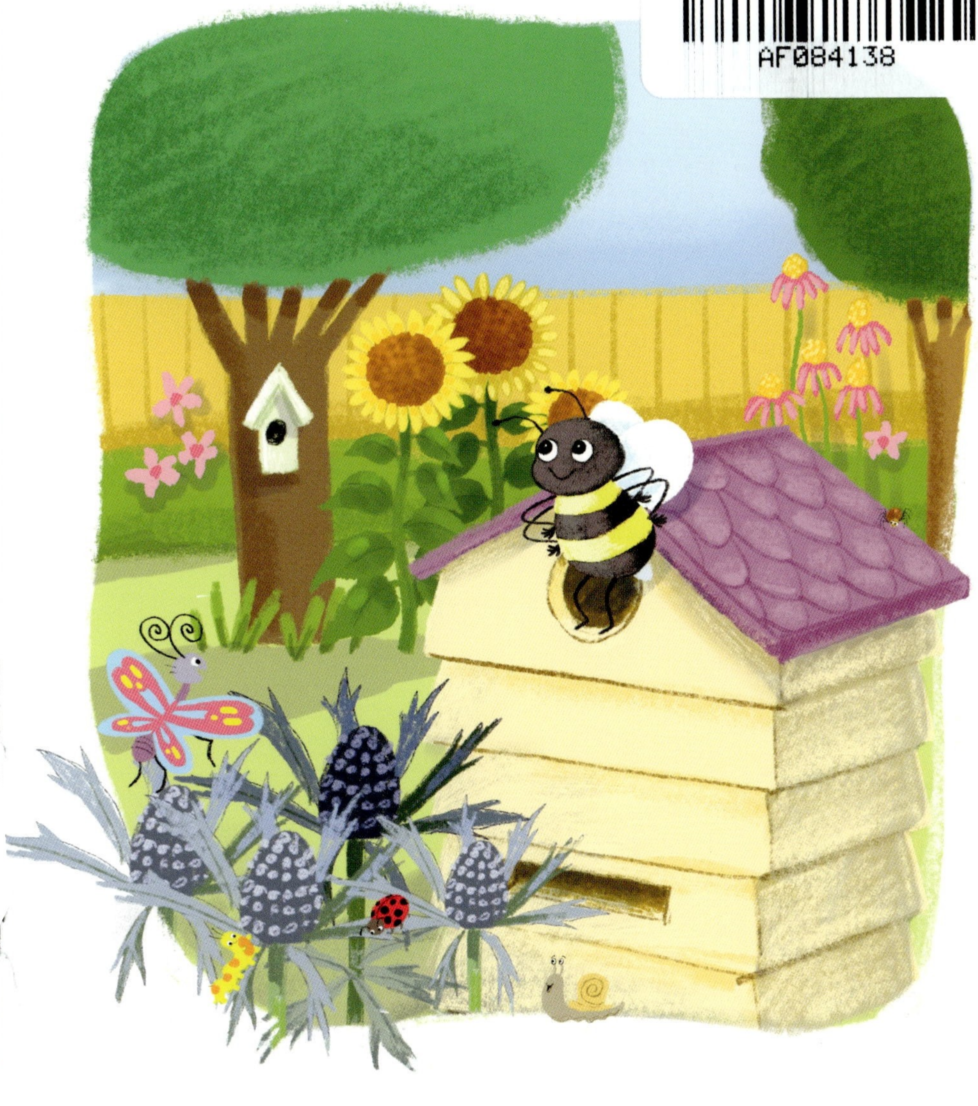

Bee!

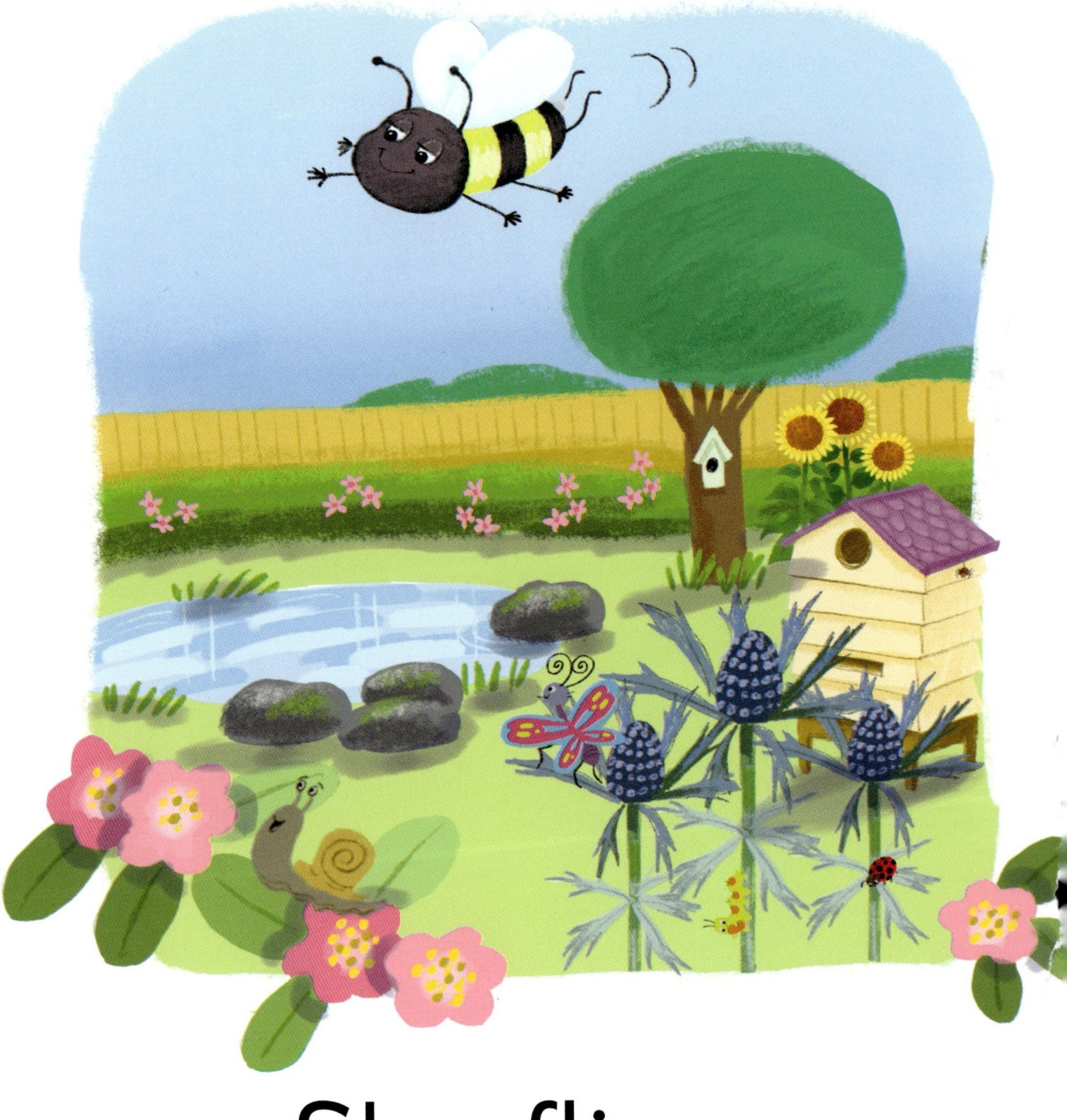

She flies...

and she zooms!

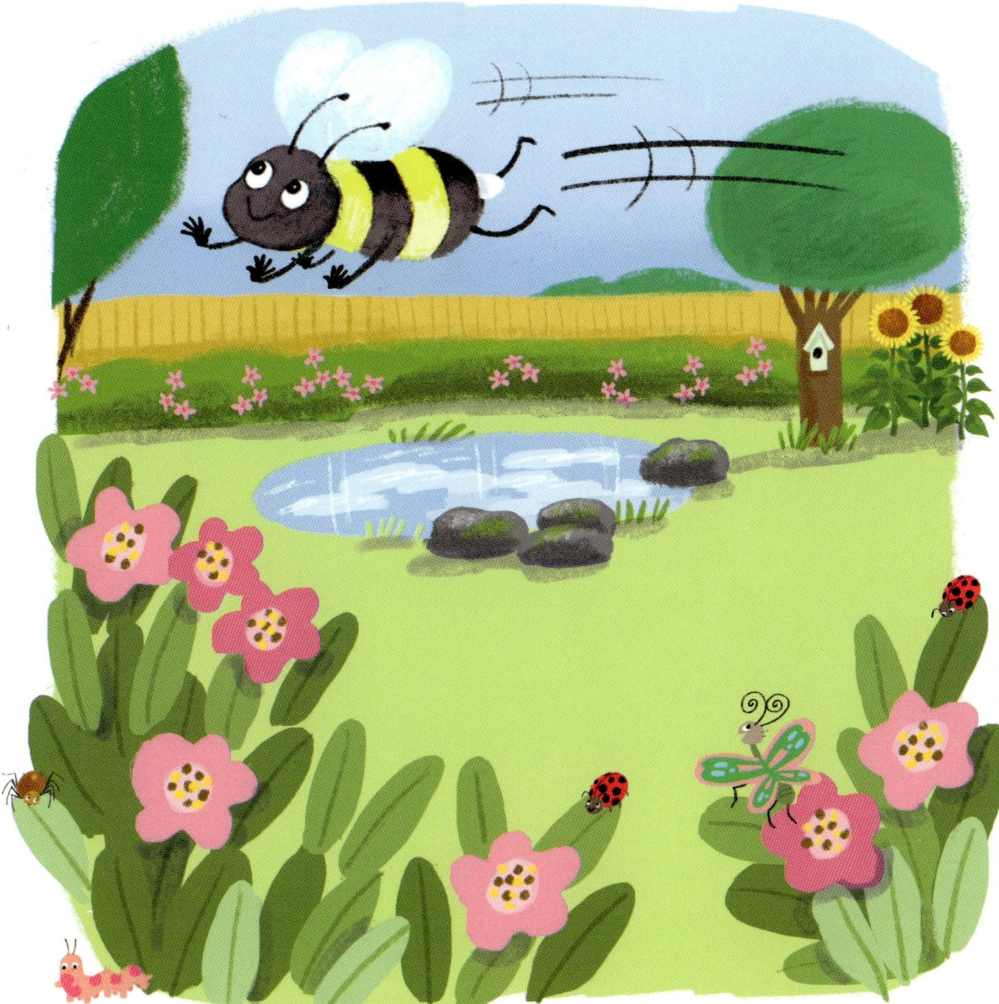

Bee lands...

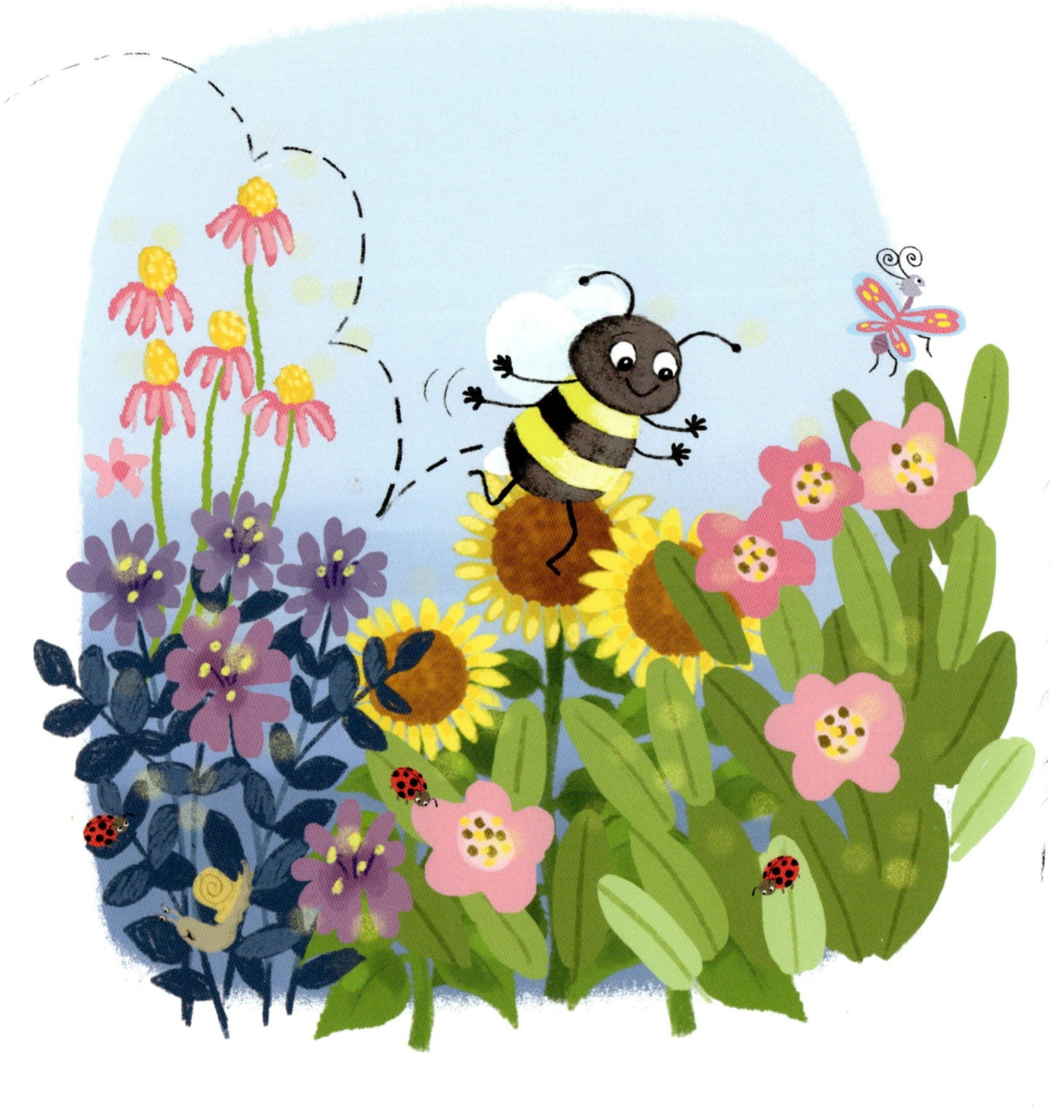

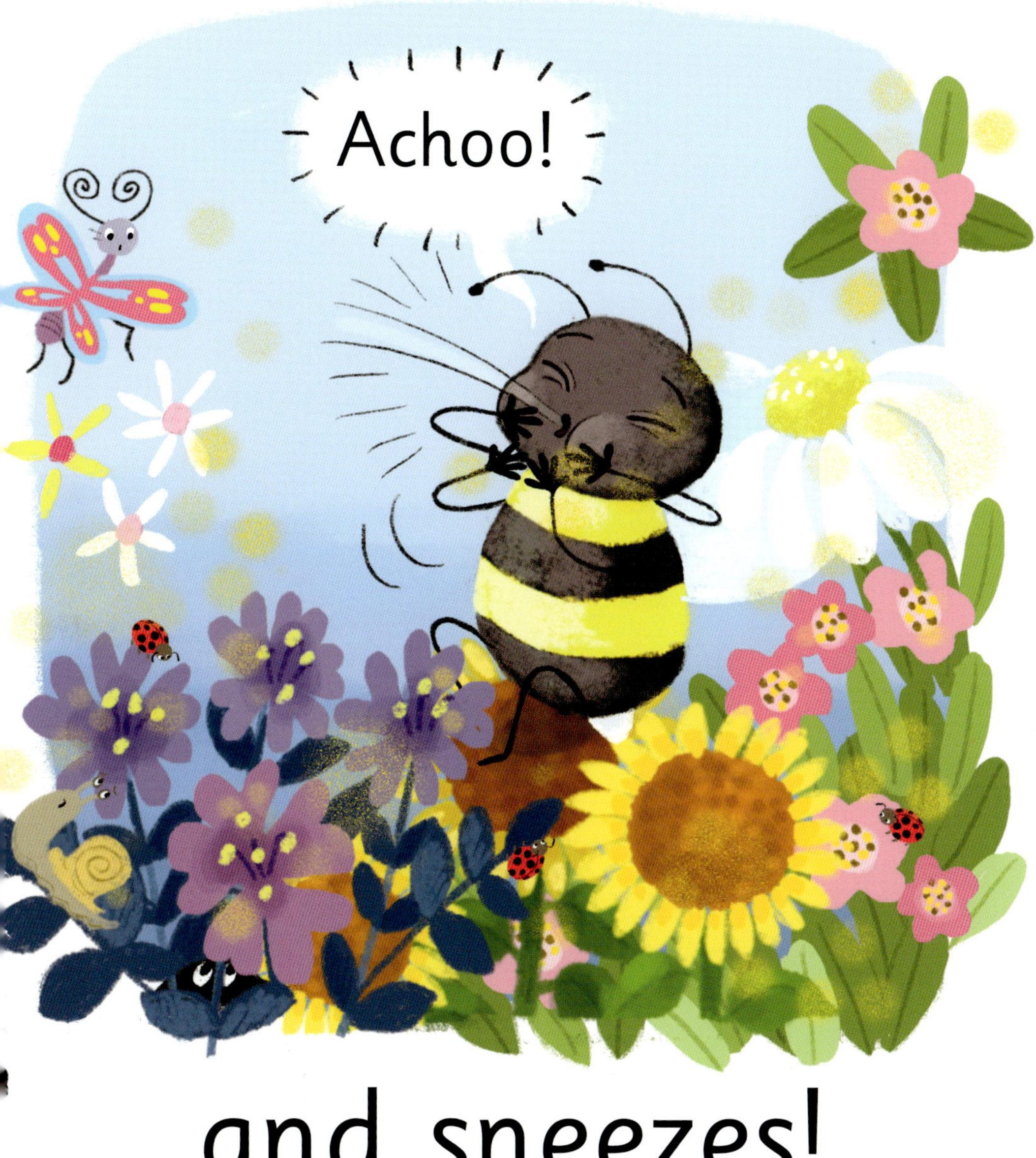

and sneezes!

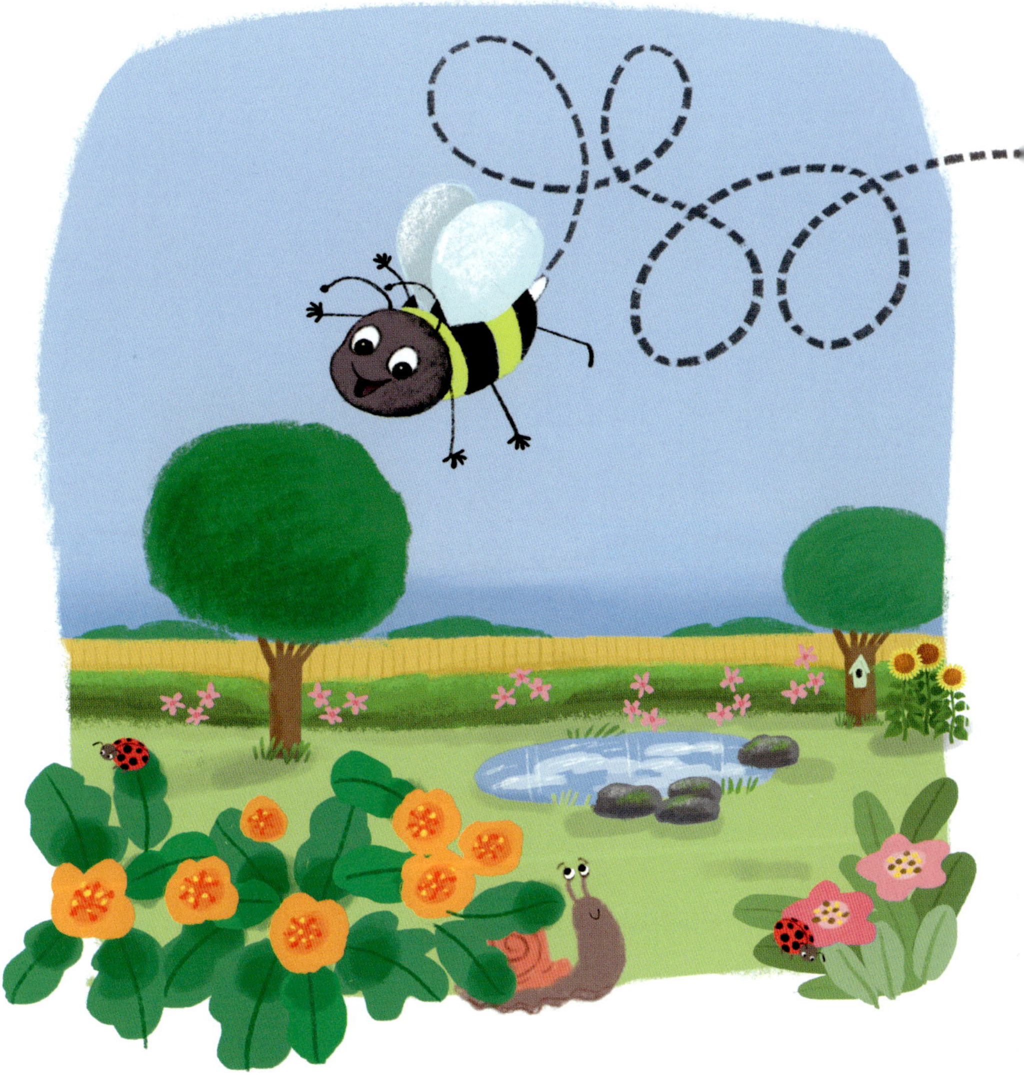

She loops

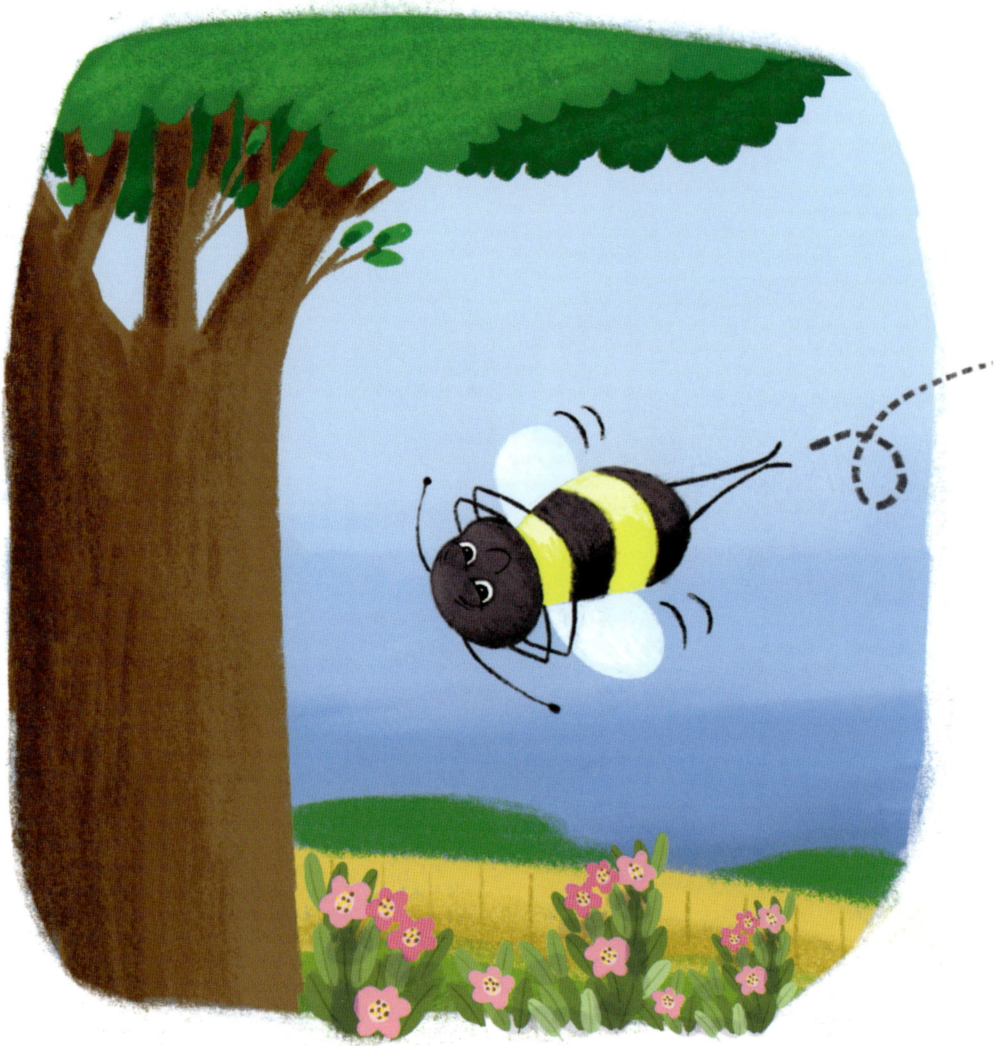

the loop...

and then...

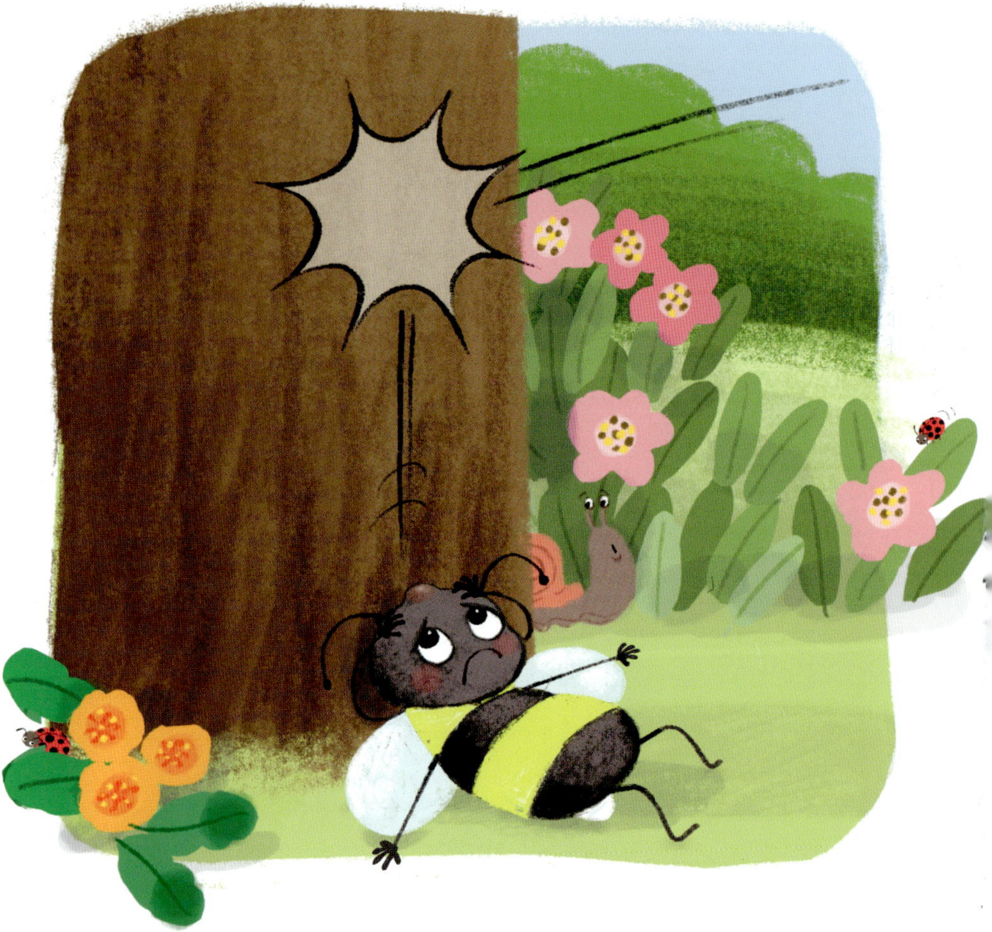

"Ouch!" she cries.